Fridolf Johnson

MYTHICAL BEASTS
COLORING BOOK

Dover Publications, Inc., New York

Preface and Bibliography

All the creatures depicted in this book are "'authentic." I have drawn them accurately, using as a guide for the appearance of each animal the details most frequently mentioned in mythology and portrayed in art. The better-known creatures, such as griffins, unicorns and centaurs, have been pictured and described so often that their "true" likenesses have been established. Others have not been so well authenticated. Confusion about their anatomies has arisen from ambiguous and widely divergent accounts. This is true of numerous beasts mentioned in Greek mythology, but is especially true of many which have been vaguely described in medieval texts and seldom, if ever, drawn. Where I found conflicting descriptions I followed the one that seemed to me to be most logical.

The winged bull has been freely copied from a photograph of a famous Assyrian sculpture. All the other drawings have been based upon extensive research into ancient writings and travelers' tales, medieval illuminated manuscripts and bestiaries, dictionaries of mythology, paintings, sculptures, rare prints and drawings. The following list of books will be of interest to people who wish to investigate further the fascinating topic of mythical beasts:

H. C. Adams, *The Wonder Book of Travellers' Tales*, N.Y., 1927.

John Ashton, *Curious Creatures in Zoology*, London, 1890. (Reprinted by Singing Tree Press, 1968.)

Thomas Bulfinch, *Bulfinch's Mythology*, N.Y., 1913. (Paperback, 3 vols., New American Library.)

Richard Carrington, *Mermaids and Mastodons*, N.Y., 1957.

Clara Erskine Clement, *A Handbook of Legendary & Mythological Art*, N.Y., 1881. (Reprinted by Gale Research Co., 1969.)

Charles Gould, *Mythical Monsters*, London, 1886. (Reprinted by Singing Tree Press, 1969.)

George Howe and G. A. Harrer, *A Handbook of Classical Mythology*, N.Y., 1947. (Reprinted by Gale Research Co., 1970.)

Larousse Encyclopedia of Mythology, N.Y., Prometheus Press, 1959.

Henry Lee, *Sea Fables Explained*, London, 1883.

Henry Lee, *Sea Monsters Unmasked*, London, 1884.

Ernst and Johanna Lehner, *A Fantastic Bestiary*, N.Y., 1969.

Peter Lum, *Fabulous Beasts*, N.Y., 1951.

Odell Shepard, *The Lore of the Unicorn*, N.Y., 1930.

John Vinycomb, *Fictitious & Symbolic Creatures in Art*, London, 1906. (Reprinted by Gale Research Co., 1969.)

T. H. White, *The Book of Beasts*, N.Y., 1954. (Paperback, G. P. Putnam's Sons, 1960).

Published in Canada by General Publishing Company, Ltd., 30 Lesmill Road, Don Mills, Toronto, Ontario.
Published in the United Kingdom by Constable and Company, Ltd., 10 Orange Street, London WC 2.

Mythical Beasts Coloring Book is a new work, first published by Dover Publications, Inc., in 1976.

DOVER *Pictorial Archive* SERIES

International Standard Book Number: 0-486-23353-7

Manufactured in the United States of America
Dover Publications, Inc.
180 Varick Street
New York, N.Y. 10014

The **AMPHISBAENA** has two heads. With one head holding the other by the neck, it can roll itself in any direction like a hoop. It stands the cold very well, and is the first creature to come out of hibernation in early spring. The ancient historian Pliny highly recommended its skin as a remedy for cold shivers.

The **BASILISK** is not large, but all flee from him because his glance and his breath are very dangerous, killing the plants he walks upon and the birds flying overhead and making a desert of every land he passes through. He hisses like a snake and can split rocks with his breath. He has a head like a cock's and a sting in his tail.

The **CENTAUR** is part man and part horse. He lives in deep forests. When not fighting, he spends much of his time hunting with bow and arrow. Symbolic of barbarism, he readily flies into a passion, although the centaur Chiron, the teacher of Achilles, had a reputation for wisdom and goodness.

CERBERUS is a monstrous dog with three heads, though some say he has as many as a hundred. He has a serpent for a tail. Cerberus guards the gate of the palace of Persephone in Hades. As the souls of the dead enter Hades, he barks at them, but if one tries to leave, he seizes it in his jaws and gives it to Pluto, King of the Underworld.

The **CHIMAERA** was a fire-breathing monster resembling a lion in the forepart, a goat in the middle, and a dragon behind. Said to have been a female, her home was in the mountains of Lycia, in Asia Minor, where she destroyed every man she met until Iobates, King of Lycia, sent Bellerophon to find and kill her.

The **CHINESE DRAGON** is not as terrible as he looks. Early in the year he comes out of a cave in the mountains, or out of water, and races through the sky, bringing the spring weather. The early Chinese worshipped the dragon and once had his picture on national flags. He is the symbol of wisdom and hidden secrets.

The **GRIFFIN** is enormous and fierce, with the head, claws and wings of an eagle and the hind parts of a lion. It builds its nest in the mountains and lines it with gold. The griffin represents the wealth of the sun—the light that turns the east into gold at sunrise. It is one of the oldest and most popular symbols in heraldry.

The **HIPPOCAMPUS** has the head and foreparts of a horse with two legs ending in fins; the rest of his body is like that of a fish. He races and frolics through the waves with great speed and is the favorite steed of Neptune, King of the Sea. Hippocampus is now the scientific name for the charming little ocean fish, the sea horse.

The **HIPPOGRIFF** was born of a mare and a griffin, having the eagle-like foreparts of a griffin and the hind quarters of a horse. It is found only in the highest mountains of the far north. Originally it was thought of as a symbol of the sun. The most famous hippogriff is the one ridden by Ruggiero in Ariosto's "Orlando Furioso."

The **HYDRA** is a dragon with many heads; when one is cut off, three new ones grow in its place. Its name comes from the Greek word for water, with special reference to the dangerous torrents of the Hydrus River in Arcadia. The Hydra of Lerna guarded the golden apples of the Hesperides, but Hercules succeeded in slaying it.

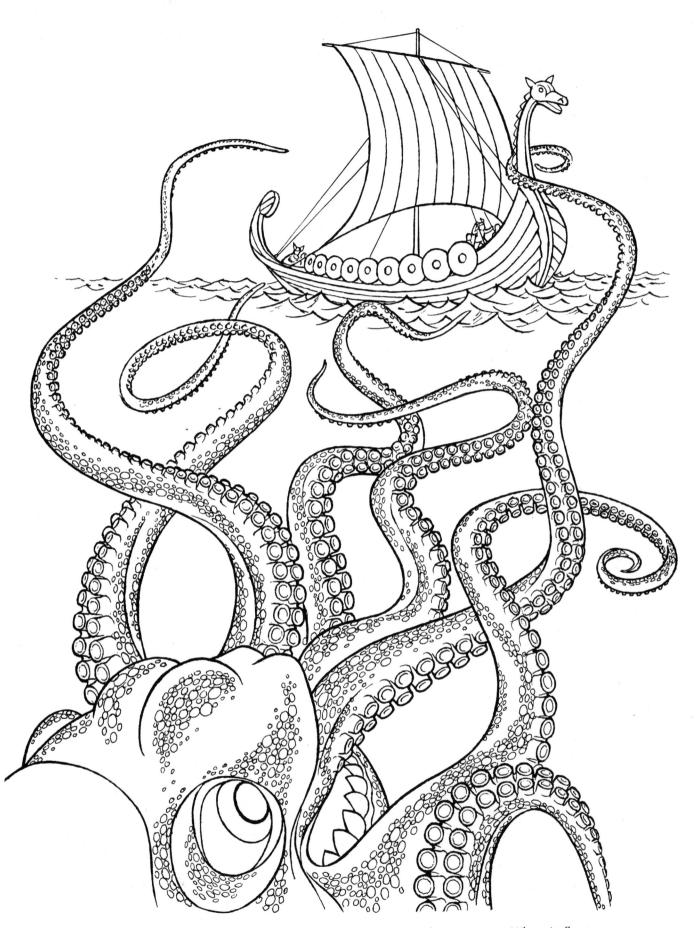

The **KRAKEN** is a huge sea monster resembling a giant squid or octopus. When it floats on the surface, mariners may mistake it for an island and land on it, only to be drowned in the whirlpool caused when the creature dives to the bottom. Sailors fear its long tentacles, which can suddenly reach out and pull a man to his death.

The **LAMIA** was named after Queen Lamia of Libya, famed for her beauty, who was turned into a beast because of her cruelty. She has the head and breasts of. a woman, and is the fastest runner in the world. Standing perfectly still, she lures men with her great beauty, then suddenly tears them to pieces. There is another lamia shaped like a serpent.

The **MANTICORE** lives in the Indies. It has the body of a lion, a spiked tail with the sting of a scorpion, a man's head with three rows of teeth and gleaming, blood-red eyes. Its shrill voice sounds much like a flute. It is very powerful and can jump great distances. It is a ravenous beast, particularly fond of human flesh.

MEDUSA was once a beautiful mortal, but Athena changed her into a monster with snakes for hair. Anyone who looked directly at her head was turned to stone. Her sisters were the Gorgons Stheno and Euryale. All had teeth and claws of brass, and wings on their backs and ankles. Perseus finally slew Medusa. The head was given to Athena, who carried it on her breastplate.

The **MERMAID,** one of the best-known mythical creatures, is often pictured admiring herself in a mirror while combing her hair. She will lure a sailor to destruction by her charm, but a man clever enough to steal and hide her girdle can make her grant any wish he chooses or take her home to be his wife. If she finds the girdle, however, she will vanish.

The **MINOTAUR** had the head of a bull and the body of a man. It lived in the Labyrinth—a maze from which no mortal could find a way out. King Minos forced the Athenians to sacrifice youths and maidens to this monster, but Theseus, an Athenian prince, killed the Minotaur and escaped by following a thread he had unwound as he passed through the Labyrinth.

PEGASUS is a beautiful and gentle horse with wings. The sacred Fountain of Hippocrene gushed from the spot where he struck the ground with his hoof on Mount Helicon. It was on the back of Pegasus that Perseus rode to rescue Andromeda from the fearful dragon. He symbolizes poetic inspiration because of his flights into space.

The **PHOENIX** lives in a sacred grove and feeds on air alone. When he is a thousand years old, he flies over the world to Phoenicia, where he builds a funeral pyre atop the tallest palm tree and sets himself on fire. Nine days later, a new phoenix arises from his ashes. This bird has long been used as a symbol of resurrection.

The **ROC** is so huge it can kill an elephant to feed its young by lifting it high in the air and dropping it to the ground, smashing it to pieces. Marco Polo wrote about it, but the most famous roc is the one described in the "Arabian Nights," in which Sinbad the Sailor escapes from a deserted island by tying himself to the roc's leg with his turban.

The **SATYR** is half man and half goat, with pointed ears and with horns growing out of his forehead. Satyrs are usually peaceful creatures, but can be rowdy companions and a threat to women because of their great fondness for love, wine and revelry. They are most often seen in the deep woods, dancing briskly to the music of their flutes.

The **SEA LION** has the head and mane of a lion and forelegs like those of a lion, but ending in webbed claws. The rest of him is shaped like a fish's tail. The beast was probably fabricated from early mariners' garbled reports of the sea lions of the seal family.

The **SEA SERPENT** has been described by Aristotle, Pliny, Olaus Magnus and many other learned men and travelers. Like the Loch Ness Monster, it appears never to have been seen entirely out of the water, at least by anyone who has lived to tell about it. It is generally thought to resemble a huge serpent with a dragon's head.

The **SIRENS** are deadly creatures similar to human beings from head to navel, but with the body and wings of a bird. Sirens flock along the wildest shores of the sea, where they sing so melodiously that unwary sailors are hypnotized by their sweet voices and, forgetting all caution, allow their boats to be dashed against the rocks.

There are two kinds of **SPHINXES:** the Egyptian Sphinx has the head of a man on the body of a lion, while the Grecian Sphinx, shown here, is a female and has wings as well. Generally associated with death, she is a mysterious creature indeed. Possessing all the deep secrets of the universe, by her eternal silence she refuses to reveal them.

TRITONS are men in the upper part of their bodies and fish in the lower. They are often seen riding on a hippocampus. At Neptune's command they blow on their conch-shell trumpets to calm the waves of the sea. They are named after Triton, son of Neptune, who lives with his father in a golden palace at the bottom of the ocean.

The **UNICORN** has the head, body and tail of a horse, the hind legs of an antelope, the whiskers of a goat and a single long horn in the center of his forehead. He lives in the forest, and runs so fast that nobody can catch him. But if a beautiful maiden waits for him under a tree, he will come to her willingly. He is often hunted for his horn, which is considered an antidote to all poisons.

The **WESTERN DRAGON,** unlike the Chinese dragon, is a terrifying beast. Somewhat like an enormous lizard, he has bat-like wings. He is the enemy of man, issuing from dark caverns to devour every creature he can find. He breathes fire; his volcanic breath can spread plagues and destroy cities. Most famous of the dragons was the one conquered by St. George.

The **WINGED BULL** was important to the ancient Assyrians. He had a man's head crowned with a horned tiara and the body of a bull with great wings. As the symbol of supernatural strength, the Assyrians often carved his image in stone to stand as guardian at the gates and doorways of their temples and palaces.

The **WINGED LION** symbolizes the conquering strength and courage of the lion combined with the wings of the eagle, which represent dominion over the entire earth. It was chosen as the symbol of St. Mark; the best-known likeness of the winged lion is the golden statue on the Cathedral of St. Mark in Venice.

The **WYVERN** is a flying creature resembling a dragon down to its two legs with their strong talons. The rest of its body is like a serpent's. Its shadow darkens the entire countryside when it flies over it, spreading great fear because it is the symbol of war and pestilence. To see one is a frightful experience.